ISBN-13: 978-0-692-39450-2

Story: Richard Warren
Illustration: Jill Fressinier

First Edition: 2013

For more information or to
order copies of this book please e-mail
the author: rtwcarmel@comcast.net

For Michael
with Appreciation

Hello Moon
for the child in all of us

Namaste

One night,
Eve woke up
and saw
the full moon.

It called to her.

"Eve."

Eve loved nature
and all things.
She felt happy to answer,

"Hello Moon."

Moon continued.

"Eve, you are a special girl.
Do you know who you are?"

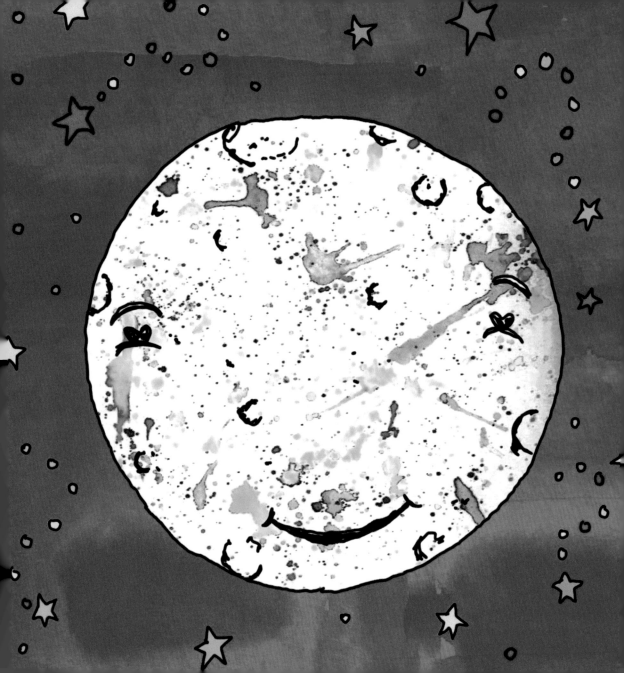

Eve thought and then replied.

"Of course I do.
I'm Eve.
I'm Seven.
I'm in second grade...

I have a brother,
Adam
and
Mommy,
Sarah...

My Daddy died in battle
and
I miss him so...

giggles!

♡ ♡

I'm taking ballet
with
my best friend Lucy...

bff

And I really love
cooking
with my Mommy."

Moon spoke again,

"Eve, you are very
wise for your age."

Moon paused
and then asked again,

"Do you know who you are?"

Eve was puzzled
and thought for a moment.

Then Eve said,

"Oh moon, of course I do.
I'm Eve, a little girl.
I live on Earth...

But I've seen the news
with Mommy.

Kids are being hurt
all over the world.

Others are hungry
and sick.
I feel so bad for them...

You see Moon,
I live in a country that's free.
I have food
and I'm safe.
I'm OK.

But Moon,
why do some kids
go to bed hungry?"

Their chat continued.
Then again Moon said,

"Eve. Do you know who you are?"

Now, Eve was getting really
puzzled by Moon's questions.
She thought again
and soon replied.

"Moon, I'm Eve. Just who
do you think I am?"

Moon took a sigh,
winked and then spoke.

"Eve, of course you're a little girl.
So right. We both know that.

But close your eyes.
Let your heart speak through you.
Tell me what you hear."

Eve trusted Moon.
She closed her eyes.
She listened to her heart.
She felt her breath come in
and speak to her.
It was a voice she knew.

Her voice spoke,
and its sound
came from her heart.

"I am air.
I am earth.
I am fire.
I am water.
I am sand and sea.
I am stars.
My home is everywhere."

Eve was bewildered.

The voice
spoke again
through her.

"I am the hungry child.
I am the orphan.
I am the nameless.
I am all suffering...

I am every child in every land...

I am
the beating heart
of all creation."

Eve
was
astonished.

Voice continued.

"I am timeless...

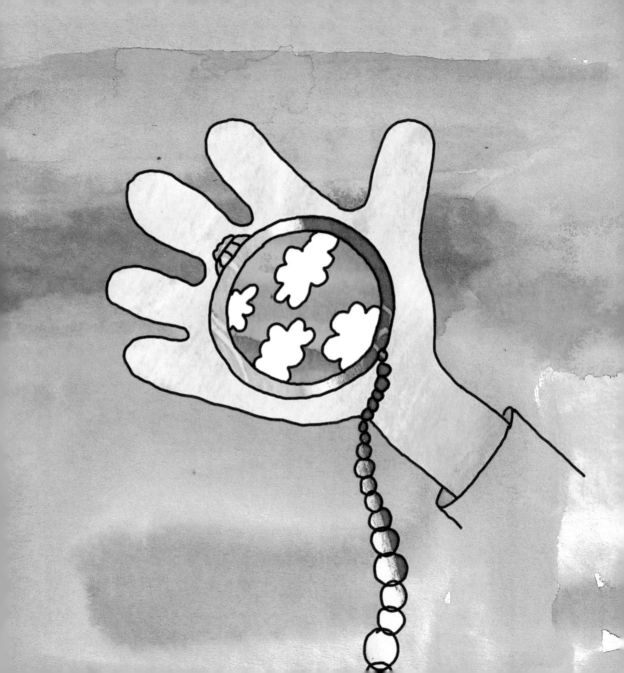

I am boundless...

I am beautiful...

I am the still voice...

and the pounding surf...

I am
the breath
of
all creation."

Eve felt these words
flowing from her heart
and she felt so alive.

She trusted her voice.

"The world needs my help,
I can make a difference."

Eve heard these words.

She *remembered* who she was.

She ran outside
and exclaimed,

"I am Eve,
a child of the stars...

I am here
to love
and
be loved.

My spirit
is
eternal."

Eve stretched her arms
up to Moon.
She felt so much love.
She was happy
and at peace.

She *knew* who she was.

And with that,
Moon winked
with
sheer delight...

and
kept winking
all night long.

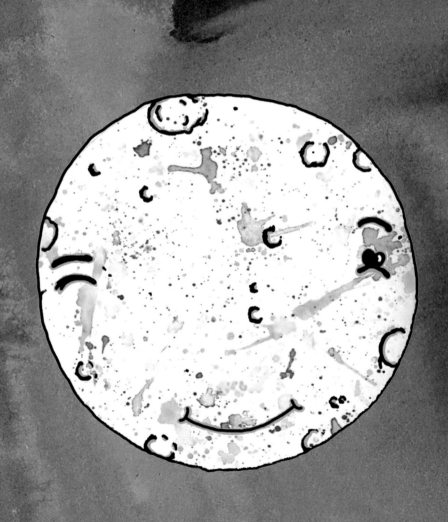

About the Author and Illustrator of Hello Moon

This is Richard Warren's first book.
He hopes its message resonates in your heart.

He lives with his wife, Barbara, on the scenic Monterey Peninsula
where he receives inspiration while
running his dog, Jacob, on Carmel Beach.

Jill Fressinier, aka "Spill", is a self-taught artist who enjoys working
in all kinds of fun mediums. Spill has owned two art galleries and
created art for everyone from legendary Indy race car drivers to
Rock & Roll Hall of Fame inductees.

She lives in the San Francisco Bay area with her husband and their
two children, and they all work in the arts,
both culinary and visual.

Richard and Spill met in Carmel-by-the-Sea,
many moons ago,
and knew that one day
they would create something out of this world together!

Jill Fressinier, artist
831/224-6098
jillfressinier @ gmail.com

Made in the USA
San Bernardino, CA
09 September 2017